Learning to Read, Step by Step!

Ready to Read   Preschool–Kindergarten
• big type and easy words • rhyme and rhythm • picture clues
For children who know the alphabet and are eager to begin reading.

Reading with Help   Preschool–Grade 1
• basic vocabulary • short sentences • simple stories
For children who recognize familiar words and sound out new words with help.

Reading on Your Own   Grades 1–3
• engaging characters • easy-to-follow plots • popular topics
For children who are ready to read on their own.

Reading Paragraphs   Grades 2–3
• challenging vocabulary • short paragraphs • exciting stories
For newly independent readers who read simple sentences with confidence.

Ready for Chapters   Grades 2–4
• chapters • longer paragraphs • full-color art
For children who want to take the plunge into chapter books but still like colorful pictures.

STEP INTO READING® is designed to give every child a successful reading experience. The grade levels are only guides; children will progress through the steps at their own speed, developing confidence in their reading.

Remember, a lifetime love of reading starts with a single step!

5 Wilder Creature Adventures!

The editors would like to thank Jim Breheny, Director, Bronx Zoo, and EVP of WCS Zoos & Aquarium, New York, for his assistance in the preparation of Wild Fliers! *and* Wild Winter Creatures!

The authors would like to thank Kaitlin Dupuis and Deanna Ellis for their help in creating Wild Cats! *and* Lion Pride!

The authors would like to thank Kaitlin Dupuis, Deanna Ellis, and Darren Ward for their help in creating Wild Dogs and Canines!

Visit us on the Web!
StepIntoReading.com
rhcbooks.com

Educators and librarians, for a variety of teaching tools, visit us at
RHTeachersLibrarians.com

ISBN 978-1-101-93917-8

MANUFACTURED IN CHINA
10 9 8 7 6 5 4 3 2 1

STEP INTO READING®

SCIENCE READERS

WILD KRATTS®

5 Wilder Creature Adventures!

Step 2 Books

A Collection of Five Early Readers

by **Martin Kratt and Chris Kratt**

Random House 🏠 New York

Contents

Wild Winter Creatures!

by Martin Kratt and Chris Kratt

Random House 🏠 New York

And . . . *brrr* . . .
we're finding out
how to stay warm with
cold-weather creatures.

Many animals live
in cold climates.
They have amazing
Creature Powers
to help them survive
in the ice and snow!

They have one or more

of the 3 *F*s.

Oh yeah,
the 3 *F*s.

FUR

FEATHERS

FAT

They help keep creatures
that live in the cold warm.

Snowy Owl!

Snowy owls have feathers as white as the snow. They keep owls warm.

Snowy owls even have
feathers on their toes.
That's really good
for standing in the snow.

Polar Bear!

Polar bears have thick coats of very warm fur. They walk in the snow, sleep in the snow, and play in the snow!

Polar bears swim
in icy water.
Then they shake their
bodies to dry out
and fluff their fur.

Walrus!

Walruses are big-bodied.
They have layers of fat
called blubber.
It keeps them warm
in icy water.

Walruses can look pink
when blood travels to their skin
to let off excess heat!

Snowshoe Hare and Ermine!

In summer, snowshoe hares have brown fur. So do ermines. The ermine is a member of the weasel family.

As winter approaches,
their fur turns white!
This helps both creatures
blend in with the snow
when they hunt and hide.

Lynx!

Lynxes have wide, flat feet
that help them run
on top of the snow.
They chase prey
such as snowshoe hares.

However, snowshoe hares *also* have giant feet, so they can run away!

Big feet don't sink into the snow.

Musk Ox!

Musk oxen have long,
shaggy fur coats
to keep them very warm.
Musk ox calves snuggle inside
the herd for extra warmth.

Musk oxen form a circle
to protect themselves
from wolves.

"Calves in the middle,"
says Chris.

"Horns out!" says Martin.

Penguin!

Penguins are covered
with smooth feathers.
The feathers keep
them warm.

These feathers also
help them swim fast
in cold water.

Penguins have to be speedy
to escape leopard seals!

Winter Birds!

Many birds fly to warmer climates in the winter. Some do not.

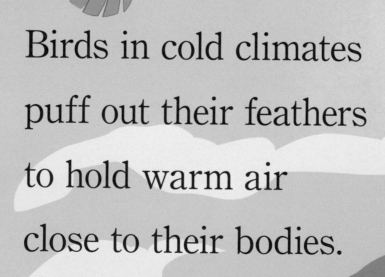

Birds in cold climates puff out their feathers to hold warm air close to their bodies.

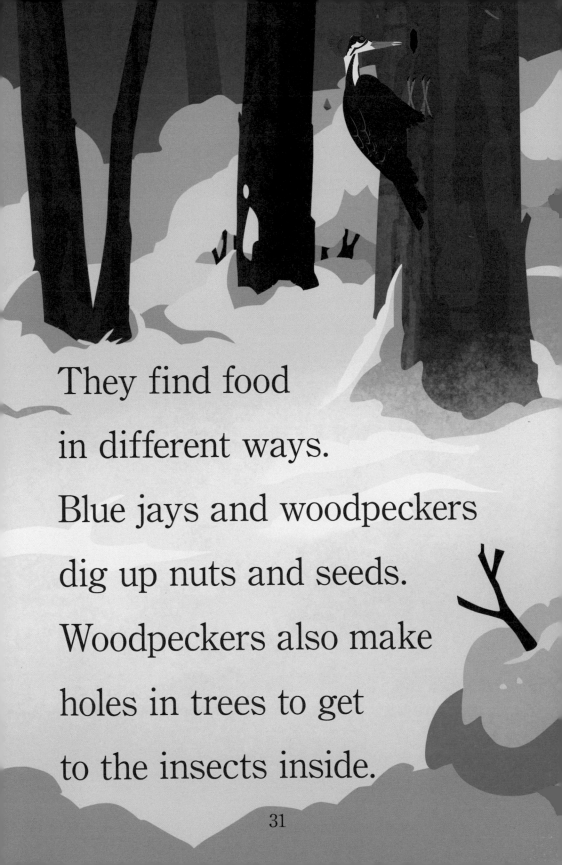

They find food
in different ways.
Blue jays and woodpeckers
dig up nuts and seeds.
Woodpeckers also make
holes in trees to get
to the insects inside.

River Otter!

River otters have waterproof fur coats to keep them warm.

In the water, they catch fish.

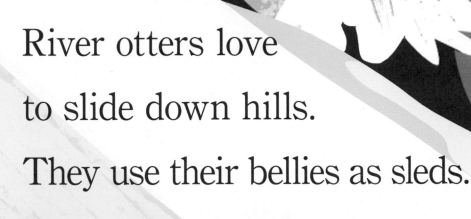

River otters love
to slide down hills.
They use their bellies as sleds.
They use a fourth F to stay
warm . . .

Fun!

Under the Snow!

Some animals use the snow for protection.

Voles and other small animals make tunnels under the snow.

There they are much safer from predators like snowy owls and lynxes.

"Whoa! This is fun,"

says Chris.

"It's like a snow fort!"

Deep Sleep!

Some animals survive by sleeping through most of the winter.

we've got to keep moving
to stay warm.
Good thing there are
always more creatures
to check out!

WILD KRATTS®

Wild Fliers!

by Martin Kratt and Chris Kratt

Random House 🏠 New York

Have you ever wished
that you could fly?
Us too!

That's why we love
to learn about
amazing animals
with the ability to fly.

The Secrets
of Flight

All animals that fly

have a special feature:

wings!

Birds have wings
with feathers.
Insects are small and
have wings made of chitin
(pronounced kite-en).

The Fastest Flier!

Peregrine falcons are
the fastest fliers in the world.
They fly high looking for
birds to chase—and eat!

When the falcon spots
its prey, it tucks in
its wings and drops.
This is called a stoop.
The Peregrine falcon can
reach speeds of about
200 miles per hour!

The Long-Distance Fliers

Monarch butterflies are beautiful insects with delicate wings.

But they are tough, too.

Every year monarch
butterflies fly
for thousands of miles.
It's a long trip called
a migration.

The Long-Distance Fliers

Many birds migrate as well.

Canada geese fly south

for the winter.

They have powerful chest

muscles that keep their

wide wings flapping.

They fly together in
a group shaped like a V.
They honk to keep
the group together.

The Hoverers

Hummingbirds can flap
their wings 80 times
a second!
This allows them to hover,
or stay in one spot,
in the air!

Hummingbirds can fly
forward and backward–
and even upside down!
They hover to sip nectar
from flowers.

The Hoverers

Dragonflies can hover, too.
They use their Flying
Powers to hunt insects . . .

and escape predators!

The Swervy Fliers

Purple martins are
amazing fliers.
They swerve and swoop
as they hunt insects:
moths, mosquitoes,
and mayflies.

Mammal Fliers

Bats are mammals that fly.
Little brown bats twist
and turn in the air while
they chase insects to eat.

Their wings are like hands with skin stretched between the long fingers.

The Gliders

Gliders don't really fly.
They jump and spread
their "wings" to take off!

A draco lizard jumps
from a tree and glides
to another tree.

Flying fish jump
out of the water
and glide on wide fins
to escape from dolphins.
They can glide for
over two hundred yards.

The Non-Fliers

Penguins are birds that cannot fly in the air. Their bodies and wings are adapted to swimming!

Penguins swim
to catch fish and escape
hungry predators,
like leopard seals.

Soaring Fliers

Soaring is when a bird
holds out its wings
and floats on rising winds.
Bald eagles soar high
in the air to search for prey.
They can see prey from
one mile away!

Turkey vultures are great
at soaring, too.
They use both smell
and sight to search
for food.

So Many Fliers

There are over one million
types of flying insects
in the world!
There are more than
ten thousand types of
flying birds!

And there are more than one thousand types of bats!

Which one is your favorite wild flier?

The Kratt Brothers agree—
with so many fantastic
wild fliers, it is very hard
to choose.

Let's fly!

STEP INTO READING®

2

STEP

READING WITH HELP

A SCIENCE READER

WILD KRATTS®

Wild Cats!

by Martin Kratt and Chris Kratt

Random House 🏠 New York

Wild Cats

Big or small, wild or tame, cats are one of the Wild Kratts' favorite predators.

Members of the cat family
are smart, fast, and strong.
And those are just a few
of their Creature Powers!

Cats Around the World

There are 38 species
of wild cats in the world.

lion

tiger

There are big wild cats,
such as **lions** and **tigers**.

There are medium-sized wild cats,
such as **lynxes** and **caracals**.

lynx

caracal

There are even small ones,
such as **margays**
and **African wildcats**.

margay

African wildcat

Cubs and Kittens

The young of big cats
are called **cubs**.

The young of medium
and small cats
are called **kittens**.

Mother cats care for their young
and teach them how to hunt.

How Cats Hunt

Cats are very good hunters.
Some cats rely on speed
to hunt. Others use
their size and strength.

Cats have sharp claws,
sharp teeth, and powerful
jaws that help them
catch their prey.

Shhh . . . quiet.
Now pounce!

Big Wild Cats

Lions live in savannas

and dry forests.

They are one of the biggest cats.

They mostly hunt big mammals, such as zebras and wildebeests. Lions often hunt in groups to take down animals that a single lion could not.

That's teamwork!

Medium Wild Cats

Caracals are great jumpers!

Their main prey is birds.

Their cousin, the **serval**,
hunts rodents
and other small prey.
Both of these cats live in
the same areas as lions.

Orange and Black Stripes!

Many types of cats have stripes, but the **tiger** is the most famous. Their stripes hide them in the forest shadows while they hunt.

Spot the Cat

Like stripes, spots help cats such as **ocelots** blend in with their surroundings.

Ocelots are very good tree climbers.

They hunt lizards, monkeys, and other small prey.

Spotted Speedsters

Cheetahs are the fastest
of all cats.
Their bodies have evolved
to run at great speeds.

Unlike most cats, their claws always stick out a little to grip the ground when they run.

We're at top speed—65 miles per hour!

Versatile Hunters

Jaguars are stocky and muscular.
They mostly live in the jungles
of Central and South America.
They hunt on land and in the water.

Leopards are lean and muscular.

They live in Asia and Africa.

They climb high into trees

to keep their food

away from lions.

Big Foot

Furry **lynxes** often live
in very cold areas.

Their big feet enable them
to run on top of the snow.

Their prey include hares, rabbits,
and other small creatures.

We have
big feet
too!

Name Game

Mountain lions live in
the Americas.
They have many habitats,
ranging from the desert
to snowy mountains.
They also have different names
in different places . . .

The **Florida panther** is a type
of mountain lion.
It has been known to clash
with another fierce predator—
the alligator!

There are less than
250 Florida panthers
left in the wild.
They may soon
disappear forever.

Some wild cats, such as
the Caspian tiger, have died out.
Bengal tigers are endangered,
and cheetah numbers are
declining.

Wild cats are amazing creatures.
Humans should try to help
wild cats survive so we can
always find them out there . . .

. . . on the prowl

and in the wild!

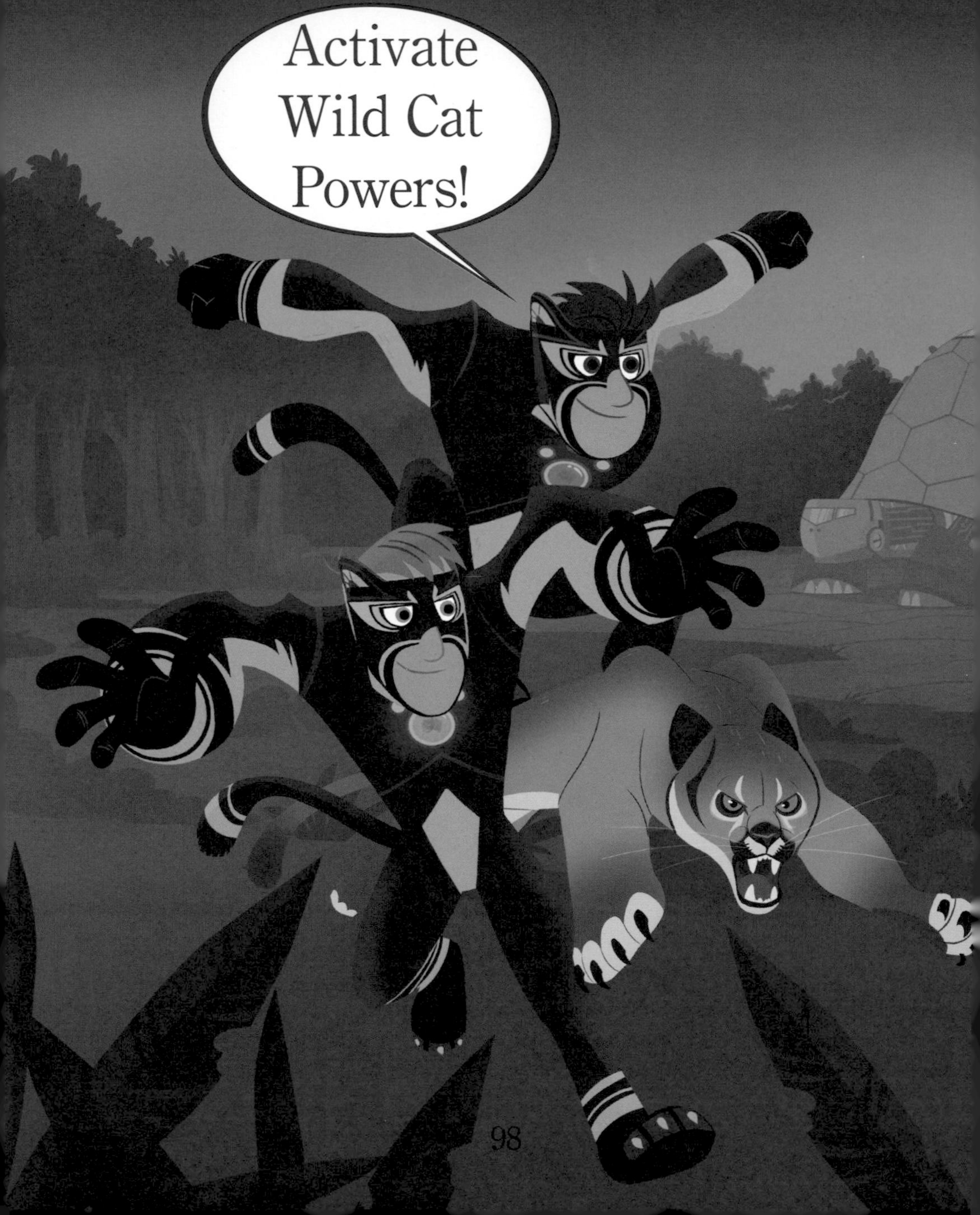

Lion Pride!

by Martin Kratt and Chris Kratt

Random House 🏠 New York

When the Kratt Brothers
go to Africa,
both Martin and Chris
love to prowl with lions.

A family of lions is called a pride. This pride has two adult males, six lionesses, and lots of cubs!

"Hey, Chris, are you thinking what I'm thinking?"

"Yeah, Martin, I think so.

Let's activate Lion Powers!"

"My Lion Power Disc is in my Creature Power Disc holder," says Chris.

"Mine is in my backpack,"
says Martin. "I think."

By the time the brothers
find their Lion Power Discs,
all the lions have disappeared!

"Where did everybody go?"
Martin wonders aloud.

Chris spots the lion cubs
gathered in the grass.

"Of course," he realizes.
"Lion cubs hide while
the adults go hunting."

Martin and Chris
quickly activate
their Lion Powers!

Insert Lion Power Discs!

Touch lions!

Activate Lion Powers!

Now that the Wild Kratts
have their Creature Powers,
Chris lets out
a roar!

The lion cubs pounce
on the Wild Kratts!
They want to play.

The brothers do not realize
that playful lion cubs
can get into a lot of trouble.

Cubs use play to practice
the skills they need
to survive in the wild.

One lion cub finds

a honey badger.

The cub gets close.

Lesson one of the savanna:

Never play with a honey badger.

Ouch!

Lesson two: Never run

under a giraffe.

You might get kicked!

Lesson three: Never play
with an elephant's trunk.
"Watch out," says Martin.

"You might get swatted,"
Chris tells the cub.

Lesson four: Be careful
on the riverbank.
Hungry crocodiles
might be waiting.

"Run back to the pride!"

Chris shouts.

Even with Creature Powers,
the Wild Kratts learn
that taking care of lion cubs
is hard work!

Finally, the adult lions
return home.
The cubs are happy
to see them.

Chris and Martin are rescued
from the playful cubs.
"Phew!" say the tired
Wild Kratts.

WILD DOGS AND CANINES!

by Martin Kratt and Chris Kratt

Random House 🏠 New York

What is found all over
the world in different habitats?
What hunts together
in pairs or packs?
Canids!

131

Canids are a group of animals that includes canines such as wolves and coyotes.

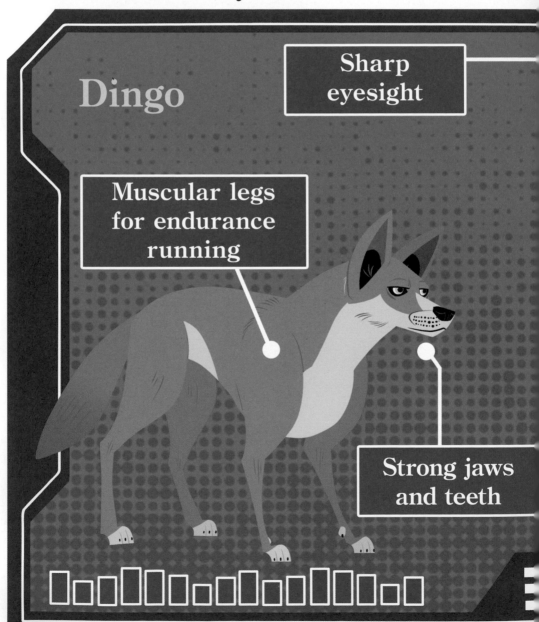

Dingo

Sharp eyesight

Muscular legs for endurance running

Strong jaws and teeth

The group also includes vulpines such as foxes. They all have many features in common.

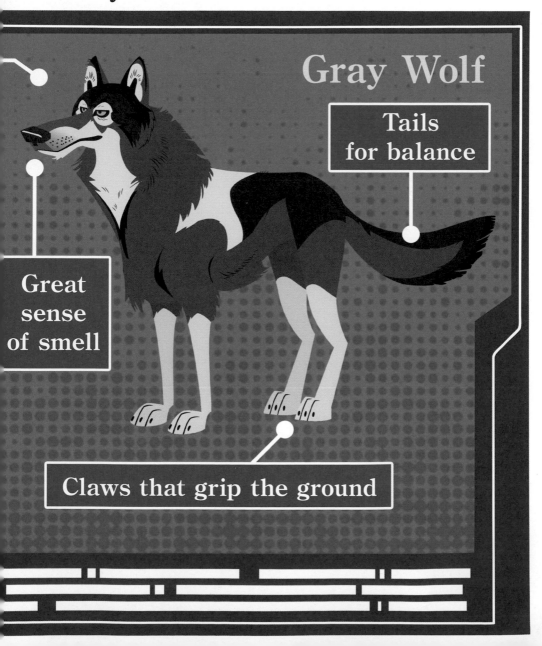

Gray Wolf

Tails for balance

Great sense of smell

Claws that grip the ground

There are about 36 different species of wild canids in the world.

"They come in many
different sizes," Chris says.
Martin suggests,
"Let's meet some of them!"

Fennec Fox!

Fennec foxes are
the smallest canids!
They live in one of the world's
biggest deserts—the Sahara!

They don't have to
drink a lot of water.
They get water from
the food they eat.

Bat-Eared Fox

Another little big-eared fox
is the bat-eared fox.

They listen for insects to eat.

Then they lick beetles and termites right off the ground. SLURP!

Yum . . . termites!

Bush Dog

The South American bush dog
is rarely seen. It can live in
burrows or hollow tree trunks
deep in the Amazon rain forest.

These tough dogs
share territory with
bigger predators
such as the jaguar!

Red Fox

These foxes live all around
the northern half of the world.
They can use their tail
to keep warm in cold weather.

Red foxes aren't always red!

They also come

in different colors,

like black or silver.

Dhole

The dhole is also called

the Indian wild dog.

Dholes are strong and fierce,

but they also work together.

A dhole pack can have 30 dogs!

Together, dholes
even take on
big predators,
such as tigers!

Coyote

The coyote is

a medium-sized canid.

Coyotes are very smart.

They eat all kinds of foods

and live in all kinds of habitats.

They survive in hot deserts,
snow-covered prairies,
tropical rain forests,
and even cities!

African Wild Dog

African wild dogs are
also called painted dogs
because each one has
a unique coat pattern.

They hunt by chasing prey
across the savanna.
While the pack hunts,
one adult always stays at
the den to take care of the pups.

Uh-oh.
Today is
my turn!

Dingo

Dingoes live in Australia.

They can hunt alone

or in packs.

They hunt both
big and small prey,
from kangaroos
to rodents!

Hop to it!

Maned Wolf

Maned wolves have
very long legs so they can
see above the tall grass
of their South American home.

Ethiopian Wolf

This is one of the rarest canids.

These wolves survive in

the mountains of Ethiopia

and eat mostly giant mole rats.

Arctic Wolf

Arctic wolves are white
and blend into the snow.
They eat small creatures,
such as mice and lemmings.

But they also use teamwork
to hunt bigger prey,
such as musk oxen.

Nice try, bro!

Gray Wolf

Gray wolves work together as a pack when hunting prey or defending territory.

They use smells, body language,
and sounds—like their
famous howl—to communicate.
A wolf pup starts to howl
when it is only eight weeks old.

Owwoooooooo!

Foxes, wild dogs, coyotes, and wolves all have amazing Creature Powers!